STORIES FROM
PANCHATANTRA
BOOK I

Retold by **Shiv Kumar**
Illustrated by **Pulak Biswas**

Children's Book Trust, New Delhi

THE MONKEY
AND
THE CROCODILE

Once upon a time a monkey lived on a rose-apple tree by the side of a river. The monkey was alone, but he was happy. The rose-apple tree had plenty of fruit all the year round. A monkey likes nothing better than rose-apples.

One day, a crocodile came out of the river and lay down near the rose-apple tree.

"Who are you?" shouted the monkey from the tree-top.

The crocodile looked up. He saw the monkey and said, "I am a crocodile from a far-off place. I am wandering about in search of food."

"Food?" cried the monkey. "I have plenty of rose-apples here. Try some. If you like them, I can give you as many as you want." The monkey plucked a few rose-apples and threw them down.

The crocodile ate them and said, "I like them very much. This is the best fruit I have ever eaten."

The monkey threw down more rose-apples and the crocodile ate them all. "May I come again?" he asked. "Will you give me some more?"

"You are always welcome," said the monkey. "Come and eat as many rose-apples as you want."

The crocodile said that he would come again. He then took leave of the monkey and went away.

The next day the crocodile came back. The monkey was happy to see him and gave him more rose-apples to eat. The monkey and the crocodile became friends.

Every day the crocodile visited the monkey. They

spent much time together. They talked about everything they knew. One day they talked about their families and friends. The monkey said he was alone and he was lucky to have a friend like the crocodile. The crocodile said that he was not alone. He had a wife and he lived with his wife far away on the other side of the river.

"You have a wife?" said the monkey. "You did not tell me that before. I would have given you rose-apples for your wife too."

The crocodile said that he would take some to his wife if the monkey wished. The monkey gave many rose-apples to the crocodile for his wife.

The crocodile went home that day with the monkey's gift. His wife liked the rose-apples very much and wanted more of them. Her husband promised he would try to get her some every day.

The monkey and the crocodile grew closer to each other and began to spend more and more time together. When they parted in the evening, the monkey always gave the crocodile a gift of rose-apples for his wife.

The crocodile's wife loved rose-apples, but she did not like her husband coming home late every day. She wanted to put a stop to it. She said one day, "I feel you have been telling me a lie. How can you, a crocodile, spend your time in the company of a monkey? He is not one of us. We always kill monkeys and eat them up."

"I am telling you the truth," said the crocodile.

"This monkey is a friend of mine. He likes me and I like him. He lives on the rose-apple tree and I go to see him every day. He gives me rose-apples to eat and he sends some to you."

"If the monkey eats nothing but sweet rose-apples," thought the crocodile's wife, "his flesh must be very sweet. He will be the most delicious dinner for me if I can only get him here." Then she said: "If you are really his friend, why don't you invite him to come home one day? I would very much like to meet him."

"No, no, I don't think I can do that," said the crocodile. "He lives on land and cannot travel in water."

"But you are his friend," said the crocodile's wife

"You just invite him. A monkey is always clever. He is sure to find a way to come here."

The crocodile was not happy about inviting his friend home. Days passed. The crocodile's wife was feeling more and more eager to eat the monkey. So she thought of a plan to get the monkey there.

One day the crocodile's wife pretended to be very ill. She began to shed tears as if she were in great pain. The crocodile was sad to see his wife ill. He sat by her side and said, " What shall I do to help you ? "

" I am very ill," said the wife. " I asked the doctor and he said that I would get well only if I ate a monkey's heart."

" A monkey's heart ? " asked the crocodile.

" Yes," said the wife, " a monkey's heart. You must get your friend's heart if you want me to get well."

" How can I do that ? " the crocodile said. " He is my only friend. I cannot think of doing him any harm."

" Then you can go and live with your friend," said the crocodile's wife. " You don't love your wife. You love only your friend. You want to see your wife dead. Then you will be free to be with your friend always."

The crocodile was very unhappy. He did not want to harm his friend. At the same time he could not allow his wife to die.

" How can I kill my only friend ? " the crocodile asked again, and started shedding tears himself.

"Why can't you kill a monkey?" said his wife. "Crocodiles have to kill monkeys."

The crocodile shed more tears; he could not decide what to do.

"You don't love me," said the crocodile's wife. "A wife cannot live without her husband's love. I have decided to end my life. When you come back today from visiting your friend you will find me dead."

The crocodile began to think. As a husband he had

to protect his wife. It was his duty. He decided to save the life of his wife. He went to see the monkey.

The monkey was wondering why the crocodile was late that day and when he saw the crocodile he asked, "Why, my friend, why are you so late? Did you meet with an accident on the way?"

"No accident," said the crocodile. "My wife and I had a quarrel. She said that I was not your friend. You have done so much for us, yet I have not invited you home. She has asked me to take you home today. She wants to meet you."

"How sweet of her to ask me home," said the monkey. "I would also like to meet her. But how can I go there? You live in water and I shall be drowned if I try to go to your home."

"We live on the river bank," said the crocodile. "I can easily take you there. You can ride on my back while I swim."

The monkey thought it was a good idea. He felt happy that he had such good friends.

The monkey and the crocodile set out for the home of the crocodile. The monkey sat on the crocodile's back, and the crocodile started swimming up the river. When they reached the middle of the river the crocodile began to dive. The monkey was frightened. "Hey," he cried. "What are you doing? I shall be drowned if you go down any further."

"I am going down further," said the crocodile. "I want to kill you."

"Kill me? Why?" asked the monkey in utter surprise. "Why do you want to kill me?"

"My wife is ill," said the crocodile, "and the doctor has said she must eat the heart of a monkey if she is to get well. You are the only monkey I know. So I have to kill you and give her your heart."

The monkey was shocked. He knew his life was in danger. He wanted to find a way of escape. He thought hard for a while and then said, "My good friend, why

didn't you tell me this before ? I would be most happy
to give my heart to save the life of your wife. But how
can I do so now ? For safety I keep my heart in a hole
in the rose-apple tree. I forgot to bring it with me. If you

had told me that you wanted my heart before we start-ed, I would have given it to you at once."

"Is that so?" said the crocodile. "Then we have to go back to get your heart."

"Yes," said the monkey, "let us go back at once and get my heart before your wife gets any worse."

The crocodile turned back and swam as fast as he could to the rose-apple tree. When they reached it the monkey jumped off the crocodile's back and climbed the rose-apple tree. He sat safely on a high branch. Then he looked down at the crocodile and said, "Now you can go back to your wicked wife and tell her that her husband is the greatest fool in the world."

THE BIG LION
AND
THE LITTLE RABBIT

There once lived a huge lion in a vast jungle. All the other animals were afraid of him, because every day he killed many of them. They feared that none of them would be left alive if the lion was allowed to go on killing them.

The animals in the jungle were very worried. They had to find a way to stop the lion from killing them. One day they all met and talked the matter over. In the end they decided to go to the lion himself and discuss it with him.

The next day, a large number of animals went to the lion. The lion roared with happiness, for he thought that he could now kill them all without having to go hunting.

"Your Majesty," said one of the animals, "we have come to ask you to hear us before you kill us. You are our King and we are your subjects. But you kill so many of us that we are growing less and less day by day. Soon, we fear, there will be no animals left in the jungle, except you. A King cannot live without subjects. When we all die, you will no longer be King. We want Your Majesty to remain our King for ever. So we have come with a humble plan. We ask you, our great Lord, to stay at home. And we shall send you every day one animal for your food. Your Majesty will not have to hunt any more. You will have enough food at home. In this way both the King and his subjects can live in peace."

The lion thought about this plan. He felt there was some sense in what the animals said.

"All right," said the lion. "I agree to your plan. But if ever you fail to send me enough food, I shall kill as many animals as I like."

The animals promised him that they would not fail to send him enough food.

From that day onwards one animal was sent to the lion every day and the lion ate him up. All the animals living in the jungle had to take turns in sending one of their kind to the lion. This went on for a long time. One day, the turn of the rabbits came. A small rabbit was asked to go to the lion. This little rabbit was a clever animal. He did not like the idea of being eaten up by the lion. He wanted to find a way to save himself

and, if possible, to save the lives of other animals also. He thought for a long time and at last decided on a plan.

The rabbit went to the lion. But he didn't hurry. He walked very slowly and reached the lion's den very late.

The lion was very hungry when the rabbit arrived and he was very angry when he saw such a small animal coming to him as food. He roared : " Who sent you here ? You are too small for my meal and you are very late. I am going to teach all the animals a lesson for sending you here. I shall kill them all."

The little rabbit bowed low and said, " O great King, please hear me. You must not blame me or the other animals for what has happened. The animals knew that one rabbit was too small for a lion's meal and so they sent six rabbits. But on the way five of us were killed and eaten up by another lion."

" Another lion ? " roared the lion again. "Who is he ? Where did you see him ? "

"It was a big lion," said the rabbit. "He came out of a big cave in the ground. He was going to kill me too, but I said to him, 'You don't know, sir, what you have done. We were all going to our King to be eaten up. Now you have spoiled his dinner. He is not the sort of king to allow such a thing to happen. He will come and eat you up. Be prepared.' He then asked me, 'Who is this King of yours?' 'Our King is the biggest lion in this jungle,' I told him. He was furious when he heard this and said, ' You know I am the only king in this jungle and all the animals here are my subjects. I deal with them as I like. The fellow whom, you say, is your king, is a thief. Bring him here and I shall show him who the real king is.' Then he sent me to take you there."

On hearing this the lion roared and roared in great anger and his roars shook the whole jungle.

" Show me the way to the place where this fool

lives," said the lion. "I shall have no peace until I see him and kill him."

"Quite so, Master," said the rabbit. "The fellow deserves to be killed. How I wish I were bigger, for then I myself would have torn him to pieces."

"Show me the way," said the lion, "show me where he lives."

"Yes, Master, please come with me." And the little rabbit led the big lion to a well in the jungle.

"Here, my Lord," said the rabbit, "he lives down here in this fortress. Be careful, an enemy in a fortress is difficult to deal with."

"Leave that to me," said the lion. "Where is he?"

"He was up here when I saw him," said the rabbit. "The moment he saw you coming, he must have jumped down into his fortress. Come, sir, I shall show him to you."

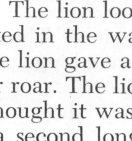

The rabbit went to the well and told the lion to look down. The lion looked into the well and saw himself reflected in the water.

The lion gave a loud roar. From the well came a louder roar. The lion heard the echo of his own voice and thought it was the roar of the other lion. He did not wait a second longer. He jumped into the well to kill the enemy.

The lion's head crashed against the rocky wall of the well. He fell into the water and was drowned. So the big lion was dead. The little rabbit returned home and told all the other animals how he had managed to kill the lion. They were all very happy that their great enemy was dead. They were grateful to the little rabbit for killing the big lion and they all said what a clever rabbit he was.

THE STORK
AND
THE CRAB

Once upon a time there was a stork. He lived by the side of a tank. There were plenty of fish in the tank and the stork had a happy time.

Years passed. The stork grew old and weak. He found it difficult to catch all the fish he wanted for his food. At times he had to go without food. He was afraid that he would soon die of starvation.

Then, the stork thought of a plan. He went and stood by the side of the tank looking very, very sad. He did not even try to catch the fish that went quite near him. The fish, frogs, and crabs in the tank noticed the unhappy stork and wondered what the matter was with him. Finally, a crab asked him: "Why do you look so sad, Uncle? Why are you not catching fish as usual?"

The stork replied, "I have spent all my life by the side of this tank. I have always been happy. There were plenty of fish in the tank and I had enough to eat. Now things are going to change. All the fish in the tank are going to die, and I shall be left without food."

"Why, Uncle," exclaimed the crab, "how can that be?"

The stork replied, "I have heard people say that they will soon fill this tank up with earth and grow things here. If they do that there will not be any fish left."

The fish, crabs, and frogs in the tank heard what the stork said. They became afraid. They all went to the stork and said, "Uncle, you have given us bad news. But you are wise. Please tell us how we can escape."

The stork said, "I am only a bird. How can I do anything against the wishes of men? However, I think I may be able to help you. I know where there is a bigger and deeper tank. They won't be able to fill that one up so easily. If you like I can take you all there."

"You are our only friend, Uncle," said the fish. "You can save us. Please take us to that tank."

"It will be very difficult," said the stork, "but I shall do my best."

"Take me first, take me first," cried every fish in the tank.

"You must be patient," said the stork. "I can take only a few at a time. But I shall try to make as many trips as possible. Remember that I am old now and I shall want a little rest after every trip."

Soon the stork set out. He took a few fish in his beak

and flew away. He did not, however, go to any other tank to let them live safely there. Instead he carried them to a big rock and there he ate them up. Then he returned to the tank. He took a few more fish, only to fly with them to the rock and make a meal of them. The stork had had enough food for the time being. He rested until he felt hungry again. Then he went back to the tank to take some more fish. He visited the tank as often as he felt hungry.

Among the fish still left in the tank was a big crab. He also felt that he should leave the place to save his life. He went to the stork and said, "Uncle, save me also from death."

The stork was now getting tired of fish and so he thought he would try crab meat for a change.

"Of course, my young friend," said the stork. "I am here to help you. Come, I shall take you to the big tank."

The crab went to him and the stork picked him up and flew away.

As the stork flew, the crab looked down to see the tank where he was going to live, but he could not see any water anywhere.

Soon the stork was flying down.

"Uncle, where is the big tank to which you are taking me?"

"Ha, ha, ha," laughed the stork. "Do you see that huge rock down there? That is where I am taking you. That is where I took all the fish."

The crab could now see the rock clearly.. There were heaps of fish bones on the rock. The crab was frightened. He knew that the stork would land on the rock, kill him, and eat him, as he had done to all the fish. The crab thought hard. Suddenly he dug his sharp claws into the stork's neck. The stork struggled, flapped his wings, and tried his best to get rid of the crab. But the crab dug his claws harder into the stork's neck and soon the stork fell to the ground. By this time, the crab had cut the stork's head right off. He dragged the head back to the tank where he had lived.

The fish in the tank were surprised when the crab came back. "Why, brother," they asked, "why have you come back? What happened to Uncle Stork?"

"Here he is," said the crab. "He is here with me, but only his head." He then told them how the stork had

tricked them and how he had put an end to him.

The fish, frogs, and crabs still left in the tank thanked the crab for killing the wicked stork, and they all lived happily ever after.

THE
CROWS
AND
THE
BLACK SNAKE

Father Crow and Mother Crow had their nest in a huge banyan tree. They had lived there for a number of years and had many children.

One day a large black snake came and made its home in a hole beneath the banyan tree. The crows did not like having a black snake as their neighbour. But they could not do anything about it.

Mother Crow laid eggs again and the baby crows were hatched. Father Crow and Mother Crow looked after them very carefully.

One day when the crows were out looking for food, the black snake crawled up the tree. He killed the young crows and ate them up. When Father Crow and Mother Crow returned, they were shocked to find their little ones gone. They did not know what had happened to the little crows. They asked all the birds and animals who lived nearby but nobody could tell them how their children had disappeared.

They cried for a long time and then decided to be much more careful when they had children again.

Months passed. Mother Crow again laid eggs and again, the baby crows were hatched. This time the crows kept watch over the children more carefully. One of them always remained at home when the other went out for food.

One day, Mother Crow saw the black snake crawling up the tree. She cried for help and tried her best to

prevent the snake from coming up. But the black snake
crept up, killed the baby crows and ate them.

Mother Crow cried and cried. Many other crows
came to her and they all cried. They tried to attack the
snake. But the snake went down into his hole before the
crows could do him any harm.

The crows were still crying when Father Crow came
home. He was also very sad when he heard what had
happened. He tried to comfort Mother Crow, but
Mother Crow was heart-broken and said, "We must
leave this place at once. As long as that black snake
lives here, we are not safe. We shall go far, far away
and make our home somewhere else." Father Crow
said, "We have lived here for a great many years. It
will be a sad thing to leave our home now."

"But," said Mother Crow, "who will protect us from
this wicked black snake?"

Father Crow replied, "We shall have to find some way to drive away the snake. We have our friend, the old fox. He is clever. Let us go and consult him."

Mother Crow agreed. They both went to the old fox and told him what had happened. " Help us ! " they cried. " Save us from this cruel snake or else we shall have to leave our home and go away."

The old fox thought for a while and then said : " You must not leave your home where you have been staying for so many years. We have to find a way to get rid of this snake. I think I can help you. Do as I

44

tell you and there is every chance that the snake will be killed. Now, listen to me. Tomorrow morning the ladies of the royal palace will go to the river to bathe. They will put their ornaments and clothes on the river bank before they go into the water. Their servants will be there some way off, and they will keep watch over the valuables.

" You go in the morning and see where they put their ornaments. When nobody is near, one of you must pick up a necklace or any other valuable thing and fly away with it. You must cry loudly so that the servants see you flying away with the ornament. They will run after you to get it back. You must fly straight to the home of the black snake and drop the ornament into it. Then see what happens."

The crows agreed to do what the fox had told them. The next morning they went to the river and waited. The ladies of the royal palace came and left their ornaments and clothes on the bank before they went into the river, exactly as the fox had said they would. The crows looked at the ornaments. They saw a pearl necklace among them. Mother Crow flew down, picked up the necklace and flew away. Father Crow followed her, cawing loudly all the way.

The servants of the royal household saw the crow pick up the necklace and fly away. They ran after the crow to get it back. The crows went straight to the

hole where the black snake lived and Mother Crow dropped the necklace into it. The servants saw what the crow had done and ran to the snake's hole. They began to look for the necklace. The black snake was

very angry and raised his hood ready to attack anybody who went near him. The servants had heavy sticks in their hands. They surrounded the snake and beat it to death. They then took the necklace and went away.

Father Crow and Mother Crow were watching everything from the tree-top. They were very happy

that the black snake was dead.
They lived happily ever after,
and were always grateful to the
old fox.

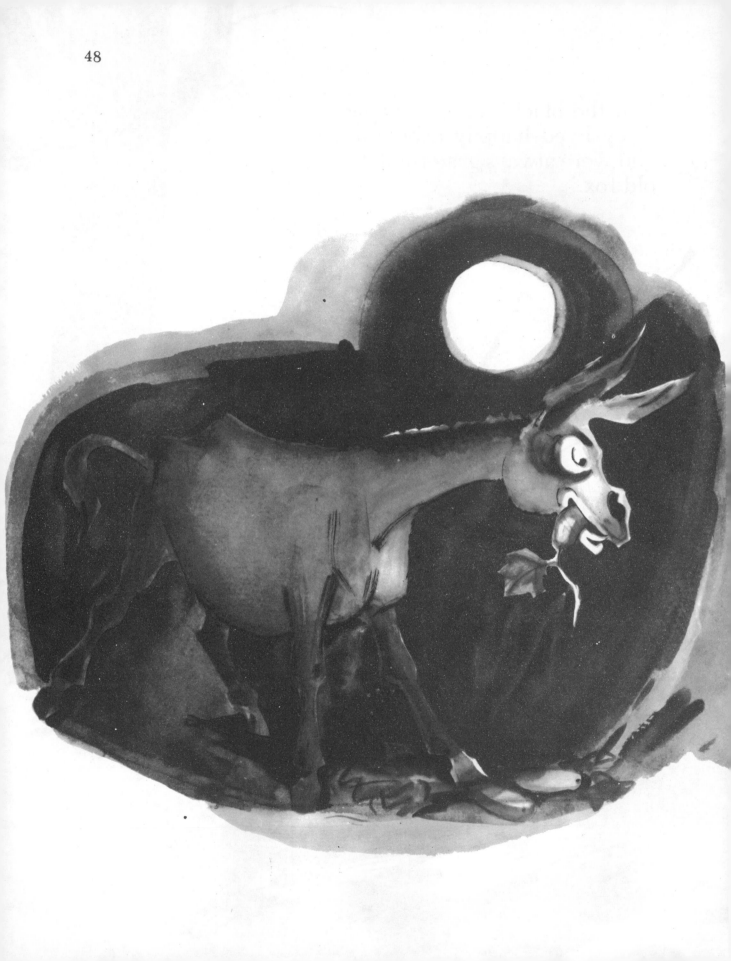

THE
MUSICAL
DONKEY

Once a washerman had a donkey. The donkey was old and lean. During the day the donkey had to carry heavy loads of clothes, but at night he was free to go about as he liked.

One night the donkey met a jackal. They became friends and wandered about together in search of food.

They found a garden full of ripe cucumbers. They went in and ate as many as they could. The next night, they went there again and ate as many cucumbers as they wanted. Thus, night after night, they visited the garden and always had a big dinner of ripe cucumbers. Soon the donkey became fat.

One night the donkey felt so happy after he had eaten, that he said to the jackal, "Look, my dear

Nephew, the full moon is shining in the sky, there is a gentle stir in the air, the night is pleasant. I feel like singing."

"Don't, Uncle, please don't," said the jackal. "It will only bring us trouble. The farmers will hear you. We are thieves here. It is better for thieves to keep quiet."

"Dear Nephew," said the donkey, "everything here is so lovely and I feel so happy. I must sing a nice song."

"No, Uncle," said the jackal, "don't sing. Besides, your voice is not very pleasant."

"You are jealous," said the donkey. "You do not like music."

"Very true, Uncle," said the jackal. "But only you can like your music. If you sing, the farmers will hear you and they will come here immediately to reward you. You may not like their reward. So you had better not sing."

"You are a fool, a big fool. Do you think I cannot sing sweet songs? Now listen to me..."

And then the donkey lifted his head to bray.

"Very well, Uncle," said the jackal. "You can sing as much as you like, but I shall go and wait for you outside the garden."

The donkey began to sing. The farmers heard his loud

braying. They knew that a donkey was in the garden and they all rushed there, carrying big sticks. The donkey was still braying when they started beating him. They hit him so hard that he fell down. The farmers tied a heavy stone mortar round his neck. Then they went away.

The donkey lay there for some time and then struggled hard to stand up. Slowly he began to walk.

The jackal was waiting outside the garden when the donkey came along, dragging the mortar with him.

"Dear Uncle," said the jackal, "so the farmers gave you a big reward for your singing. Congratulations."

"I am sorry, Nephew," said the donkey, "that I did not listen to your words of advice."

THE TORTOISE AND THE GEESE

Once there was a tortoise in a large tank. He had two geese as friends.

The geese used to come to the tank and the three of them spent much of their time together. They lived thus happily for a number of years.

Then there was a drought in the country; for a long time there was no rain. Rivers and tanks began to dry up.

There was famine in the land. There was no food. People and animals were dying. Birds were flying away to places of safety.

The two geese saw the danger from the drought, and they decided to go away to some other place.

They went to the tortoise to take leave of him.

"Why do you bid me farewell?" said the tortoise. "Am I not your friend? Don't you want me to live too? Why do you leave me here to die?"

"How can we help you?" asked the geese. "We can get to any place on earth by flying. But you can't fly."

"It is true that I cannot fly like you," said the tortoise, "but you can help me. Take me with you."

"How can we do that?" said the geese.

"That is easy," said the tortoise. "Bring me a stick. I shall hold the middle of the stick with my teeth. You can hold the two ends of the stick in your beaks and fly up, taking me with you. Then we can all fly to some place where we shall be safe from this drought."

The geese thought the matter over and said: "We hope we can do that, but there is one danger. If, by any chance, you begin to speak while we are up in the air, you will lose your hold on the stick and fall down and be crushed to death."

"But I will do no such foolish thing," said the tortoise. "I will not utter a word as long as we are in the air."

So, the geese brought a strong stick and held it in their beaks, one at each end. The tortoise held the middle of the stick firmly in his mouth.